Lots of
love
from Anuty. Moolae,
Uncle David

Christmas 2005.

# THE TURKEY AND THE BABY

# THE

# TURKEY AND THE BABY

## A CHRISTMAS STORY

by

RALPH ROCHESTER

with illustrations by
TIM MAJOR

CORVO BOOKS
LONDON
MMII

First published in Great Britain in 2002 by
Corvo Books
34A, Highbury Hill,
London, N5 1AL.

A catalogue record for this book is available from the
British Library.

ISBN: 0-9543255-0-8

Printed by
R. Booth (Bookbinders) Ltd of Mabe, Cornwall.

*For Sophie,*
*who likes her rhymes ruthless.*

# I

## THE NANNY AND THE COOK

ALL through the brief Edwardian Age
when family-life was all the rage,
that is to say, I'm sure you know,
about a hundred years ago,
there lived, at 14, Gloucester Square,
Sir Hugh and Lady Hertford Hare.

The Hertford Hares had two fine boys,
the kind who make a lot of noise,
called Jack and Bert, a girl as well,
a pretty child named Annabel.
They kept a cook, one Mrs Bold,
and nursery-maid,  old Marigold.

Thereto some maids and servants male,
who play no part in this strange tale,
and little Orphan Ben, whose rôle
was helping cook and fetching coal,
Rover a pup, and Algernon,
a parrot from the Amazon,

and two white mice called Max and Molly,
a guinea-pig called Roly-poly,
a rabbit who was far from tame,
a kitchen-cat without a name,
and Princess Maude, the parlour-cat
and one new baby, very fat!

This happy household jogged along
and not too much went very wrong
until one fateful Christmas morn
soon after Baby had been born,
when first to rise, despite the cold,
was dear old Nanny Marigold,

who, having peeled off Baby's clothes
and cleaned it up and wiped its nose
and powdered it and pinched its cheek
and kissed its feet to make it squeak,
looked up and saw a friendly grin
as Mrs Bold, the cook, came in.

This Mrs Bold, like all good cooks,
was somewhat buxom in her looks.
Her stockings were like pillow-cases
and all her bulging, curvey places
bounced like balloons. She had huge hips
that made you think of sailing ships.

Her fat red face was like the sun.
Her smile was wide and full of fun
and when she laughed her chest and belly
went wibble-wobble like a jelly,
but when she thundered, God forfend!,
you'd think the world was going to end.

Contrariwise the children's nanny,
old Marigold, was somewhat skinny
and, sad to tell, young Bert and Jack
would call her names behind her back
like *Skinny Liz* or *Lanky Letty*
or *Needle-knees* or *Beanpole-Betty*.

So when you looked at these two women
you'd hardly think they'd  much in common,
and yet they were the very best
of friends and shared an interest
in dances, music-halls and frolics,
and guardsmen from the Knightsbridge barracks.

And many virtues too they shared
for both had gen'rous hearts and cared
for bird and beast and young and old,
and often Cook gave Marigold
a bag of odds-and-ends of rations
to smuggle out to poor relations.

And good Sir Hugh was not aware,
nor yet was Fanny Hertford Hare,
how Marigold and Mrs Bold
would bring in guardsmen from the cold
and cheer each chosen, gallant guest
with steaks and ale, the very best.

And many a starveling dog came there,
to number 14 Gloucester Square,
to beg its bowl of lights or liver,
nor even pavement pigeons ever
missed out on nuts or bacon-rind,
these worthy servants were so kind.

It's true that they were now and then
less kind to little Orphan Ben
whom Nanny called a common type
and whom the cook called *guttersnipe*
and *ragamuffin* and at times
she found some even choicer names.

They clipped Ben's ear when he was slow
at lighting fires or clearing snow,
but in all households there must be
some discipline, don't you agree?,
so if they cuffed him once or twice
why!, that was virtue, not a vice.

Of vices shared there was but one,
which, though it won't be dwelt upon,
had consequences, as you'll see,
for this pathetic history.
It was a small but fateful sin:
They both were far too fond of gin!

## II

## THE BABY AND THE TURKEY

"A Merry Chrismis, Marigold!"
were the fond words of Mrs Bold,
"and see'ng as how it's Chrismis Day
I thought I'd just pop up to say
how's in my kitchen there's a gill
of gin that me and you might swill.

"So fetch that baby on your arm
down to the kitchen where it's warm
and feed it there, and while we're doin'
we'll sink a drop of mother's ruin!"
"Right y'are Martha!" said the nanny
and clasped the baby to her pinny.

"Her Ladyship's so very kind
I'm sure," said she, "she'd never mind,
an' see'ng as how it's very clear
that Chrismis comes but once a year
and see'ng as gin keeps out the cold,
I thanks you kindly, Mrs Bold."

The kitchen won, they sat within
and joked and chatted, sipped their gin
and fed the babe till it grew drowsy
then set it down all warm and cosy
upon a table, next the bird
that Cook had lovingly prepared.

A turkey! Yes! The cook had found
the finest bird for miles around,
had cut its head off and its feet,
had plucked it, cleaned it, laid it neat,
salted and peppered legs and wings
and stuffed it full with all good things.

Bird to the left, babe to the right,
each naked as the moon at night,
each with its podgy legs held high,
each pink and pleasing to the eye.
You might have thought, if you'd have seen them,
there wasn't much to choose between them.

Yet how could any woman make
so fundamental a mistake
as to pick up that bird and on it
set the baby's winter bonnet,
then squeeze that turkey's legs and wings
into the baby's lacy things,

then lift that turkey fully dressed
and clasp it firmly to her breast
and pat its back and smooth its clothes
and chuck its pretty parson's nose?
How could a nurse be so beguiled
to think a turkey was a child?

And yet, alas!, it must be told,
just such a one was Marigold.
She sat the turkey on her knee
and rocked it somewhat carelessly
and even thought she saw it grin.
And why?  Because of too much gin!

But see!  Another dreadful thing!
The cook, who had begun to sing,
had fetched and greased a roasting tin
and put the sleeping infant in,
together with shallots, tomatoes,
bacon, sausage and potatoes.

How could a cook be so mistaken
to think that she might roast with bacon,
with sausages and all the rest,
with lumps of butter on its chest,
a little child, as good as gold,
a baby barely three months old?

And yet, alas!, there is no doubt,
that's just what this cook was about.
She raised the roasting tin with care
and bore it to the oven where
she shoved the wretched baby in.
And why? All on account of gin!

# III

## SIR HUGH AND LADY FANNY

NOW while bibacious Mrs Bold
and poor, gin-pickled Marigold
were still confusing babe and turkey,
the upstairs children, bright and perky,
had leapt from bed to greet the day
and learn what gifts had come their way.

And Father Christmas must have found them
for presents tumbled all around them
and what a noise those boys were making,
enough to set the nurs'ry shaking;
and gentle little Annabel
was making quite a row as well.

Sir Hugh and Fanny Hertford Hare,
snug in the bed they liked to share,
were woken by the raging noise
of one small girl and two small boys
rampaging just across the way.
Was this their peace on Christmas Day?

The noise was getting worse and worse.
"I think it's time we sent for Nurse,"
said Lady Fanny to Sir Hugh
and rang her bell and shouted, "Sue,
tell Nurse to come at once and maybe
she would like to bring our baby."

At length the nurse tripped up the stair,
looking a touch the worse for wear,
and placed the turkey, which we know,
wore Baby's clothes from top to toe,
into the arms of Lady Fanny,
who hugged and kissed it. "Thank you, Nanny!"

What glorious smiles the mother smiled!
"My child!," she sighed, "My darling child!
How sound you sleep, my little love!
But Nanny wants you back, my dove!"
And, smiling still, my Lady gave
the turkey back, but then looked grave.

"Now Marigold, you really need
to calm those children. Why not feed
them now, at once, then take a walk.
You know how much they love the park.
And see that Jack takes his new boat.
I'm sure he'd wish to see it float.

"Take Baby too, to taste the air,"
said fragrant Fanny Hertford Hare,
"and Bert, who'll doubtless want to take
his hoop; and walk them by the lake
where Annabel may feed the duck;
and don't come home till one o'clock!"

As soon as Marigold withdrew
to do as she'd been told to do,
Sir Hugh, who'd had to hide his head
and skulk beneath the feather-bed
to save the blushes of their nanny,
could speak again to Lady Fanny.

"Well done!," said he "She'll quell that riot,
and then we'll have our peace and quiet."
"Yes," said his spouse, "I'm sure we will
and yet, my love, what frets me still…"
Here Fanny made a pretty *moue*,
"I think our baby tastes of stew!"

"Of stew!," said Hugh, "That can't be true!"
"My dear!," said she, "I'm telling you
that when I kissed our baby's cheek
I seemed to catch a smatch of leek,
of sage and onion, pepper maybe.
Believe me!, all's not well with Baby!"

# IV

## THE NANNY AND THE SERGEANT

THE sky was blue, the day was cold,
into the park came Marigold,
perambulator to the fore.
She had been careful to make sure
the turkey would be safe and warm
and could not come to any harm.

To this end she had tucked it in
and pulled soft blankets to its chin,
that is, to where she'd tied the bonnet.
She lavished words of love upon it,
sweet-nothings which, you may be sure,
no-one had told that bird before.

Behind her in his Sunday coat
came Jack who carried his new boat,
a yacht so tall, with sails so wide,
that most of Jack could not be spied.
At Jack's side was the children's puppy
who bounced along he was so happy.

Next Annabel, as sweet as honey,
whose clever ways and smile so sunny
made strangers wink at her and laugh,
frisked through the park like any calf,
singing a charming nursery song
in German as she skipped along.

And last came Albert with his hoop,
who'd lagged behind this happy group
to let his hoop fall to the ground.
He liked th'accelerative sound,
how it went *bim-bam-bim* until
at last it stopped and lay quite still.

At length towards the Serpentine
this cheerful column did incline
where Nurse met Sergeant Tammy Shand,
a Coldstreamer and favoured friend,
who walked her to a sheltered bower
and kept her there for half an hour.

With one hand Nanny rocked the pram;
her other hand she gave to Tam,
who stroked it gently while he told
wild tales of war to Marigold.
In Scottish accent loud and shrill
he gave account of Wagon Hill.

"Lassie, ye'd no believe," Tam said,
"the way our men and horses bled.
Nae woman could hae borne the sicht
and maist men would hae deid of fricht
but Coldstreamers like me ye ken
hae braver hearts than ither men."

At this point Nanny thought she maybe
ought to take a peek at Baby.
She picked the turkey up but quickly
set it down. "This child looks sickly!"
She pulled its bonnet off and then
she screamed and stuck it back again.

Too late!, the sergeant's falcon eye
had seen the turkey. With a cry –
"What horror's here?  All cold and deid!
A poor wee bairn without its heid!" –
Bold Sergeant Shand fled like the wind,
nor did he stop to glance behind.

# V

# THE CHILDREN AND THEIR KING

POOR Marigold was in a spin.
This was what came of drinking gin.
Here was the turkey, that was clear
but where was Baby if not here?
She scratched her head. What had she done?
She must go home, but not till one!

Meanwhile the boys and Annabel
were playing tag when, strange to tell,
three grave, distinguished gentlemen
strolled up across the grass and then
stopped by a tree and called them over.
The children came and so did Rover.

One of these gentlemen was tallish
and one was bearded, stout and smallish
and one was holding in his hand
a camera with patent stand
which now he set upon the ground
while his companions stood around.

"Hello!," said Albert, "Who are you?"
The tall man smiled "How do ye do?
My name is Balfour and, young sir,
I am your King's first minister."
The bearded man said, "That's the thing!,
and we are Edward. We're your king!

"And this is Mr Butterworth
who's here to take our photograph
and we were hoping that you three
might stand beside our royal knee.
Just think, in next month's *Strand* you'll find
your picture. That's if you don't mind."

"No, we don't mind," said Annabel,
"but, please, our nurse is here as well
and so is Baby.  Couldn't you
put Baby in your picture too?
I know our mother would agree,
it should be all the family."

The men looked hard at Marigold.
"No, not the nurse.  She's far too old,"
said Mr Balfour to the king.
"That baby though is just the thing,
and if, Sire, you could kiss the brat,
the nation would rejoice at that."

Poor Marigold, she blushed and sweated.
She gave her king the bird then fretted.
Perhaps his nibs would find her out.
She cringed.  She feared a royal shout.
The king, however, kissed the child
while Mr Balfour smiled and smiled.

"Thank you!," said Mr Butterworth,
"I think we have our photograph."
"Take down this child!," the king said, coughing,
"It tastes unwashed and smells of stuffing."
Said Mr Balfour, still he smiled,
"God bless and keep thee, pretty child!"

The bird was back and in its pram.
The king said, "Farewell little lamb!"
Old Marigold had curtsied low
and blessed him as she saw him go,
then, gath'ring up her little flock,
she drove them home for one o'clock.

# VI

## THE FAMILY FEAST

THE dining-room at Gloucester Square
gleamed bright where Fanny Hertford Hare
was placing crackers on the table
helped by a serving-maid called Mabel.
The children came and took their places.
You never saw such shining faces.

Sir Hugh, of course, was there as well
and grace was said by Annabel
and then came the *hors d'oeuvre* which was
a cheese tart *à la Franc Comtoise*
which, being ate to the last crumb,
made way for better things to come.

Enter the dish, the family cheered.
The lid was raised. The bird appeared,
appeared at least to be a bird
but not a turkey all averred.
A goose perhaps! It smelled divine.
A servant came and poured the wine.

"A happy Christmas ev'ry one.
I wish you all a feast of fun!"
Sir Hugh had carved and shared the bird,
'twas he who spoke this festive word.
The family drank with good Sir Hugh,
filled up their plates and then set to.

When all had fed, the bird was gone;
only the smell still lingered on.
The bits and bones that were left over
were sent down as a treat for Rover.
Said all, "Where's Cook? We must reward her.
Congratulations are in order."

They sent for Cook.  She did not come.
Back came young Mabel looking glum.
"There ain't no sign of Mrs Bold,
Your Ladyship, nor Marigold.
It must be them what wrote this note.
They left it in the gravy-boat."

The note was opened and was read
and word for word here's what it said:

*Dear Lady Fanny,We has gone.*
*How could we bear to carry on?*
*Your baby's been sent up.  It's plated.*
*We hopes you hasn't been and ate it.*
*We blames the gin. We lost our touch.*
*That second bottle was too much!*
*That's why we mixed up what was which.*
*That's how we came to make the switch.*
*Your child's in heav'n. You'll see it never.*
*Your turkey should be good as ever.*

The Hertford Hares have read the note.
Her Ladyship has clutched her throat.
"Goodness!," she cried, "They've run away.
How come good servants never stay?
But what is worse, it seems that maybe
our Christmas feast was mainly Baby."

Poor Lady Fanny's looks were wild.
How could one stomach one's own child?
Up jumped Sir Hugh, the children too.
"O dear!," they cried, "What shall we do?
We must conclude,  we can't avoid it,
we've ate our baby and enjoyed it."

# VII

## THE ORPHAN'S TALE

WHO knows what might have happened next?
The Hertford Hares were apoplexed.
They found the thought quite flabbergasting
that they were inwardly digesting
their smallest member, but just then
piped up the voice of Orphan Ben.

The ragged boy stood near the door
where he had never stood before.
Until that day he had not dared
to leave the kitchen and the yard.
His face was black. His eyes were red.
His smile was startling and he said:

"Cheer up you lot, for I have got
good news. Your baby's in its cot,
as right as rain and twice as happy.
I've fed it twice and changed its nappy.
And if you don't believe, come see!
Don't hang about! Just follow me!"

The Hertford Hares all ran like smoke
up to the nurs'ry. What a joke!
With what delight did they discover
their smallest one as fat as ever,
and O, how sweet its foolish prattle!
What bliss to see it swing its rattle!

The baby looked as pleased as Punch
not to have been their Christmas lunch.
The father clasped it to his chest,
the mother to her heaving breast;
then all went down, at Mabel's bidding,
to table and to Christmas pudding.

Ben was the hero of the day.
Sir Hugh insisted that he stay
and sat him down and fed him up
and Ben drank from a silver cup
the ruby wine, and then he told
about the bird and Mrs Bold.

"Ladies and gents, you might not know,
but there's a coal-house down below,
that's where we sleeps, all damp and cold,
me and the cat.  And Mother Bold
most mornings wakes us up before
the sun has reached your coal-house door.

"Today though, Cripes!, I sleeps in late
and when I wakes I'm in a state.
I thinks I'd better jump up quick.
I grabs some paper and a stick
and pops in through the kitchen door
an' then I hears a pow'rful snore.

"It's Mother Bold and she's been drinkin'
The bottle's empty and she's stinkin'
of gin.  I shouts and tries to shake her
but nuffin human's going to wake her,
so I shoves off and strikes a light
and fires the oven, hot and bright.

"I'm pow'rful hungry, so before
I leaves I tries the oven door
'cos sometimes I finds scraps of meat
or burnt potatoes there to eat.
I stretches in as far it goes
and, Cripes!, I'm ticklin' Baby's toes.

"I hoicks that tin out in a minute
and there's your baby sittin' in it
as naked as the kitchen-cat.
I picks it up.  It's pow'rful fat
and heavy, so I finds some clothes
and lays it in its cot to doze.

"And then I thinks, the family
will need to eat. There's Mrs B.
still snorin' like a pig in clover
and so I goes and fetches over
the goose what she's had put away
intending it for New Year's Day.

"I sticks that goose into the tin,
the one your baby's just been in,
and builds the fire up very hot
and back it goes, the bloomin' lot.
Now that's wound up. There ain't no more.
Cripes!  Don't this talkin' tire the jaw!"

"But why, dear Ben," said Lady Fanny,
"did you tell none of this to Nanny
or Mrs Bold?...."  But good Sir Hugh
had heard enough.  "There's no need to
interrogate the boy, my sweet.
He's saved our baby and our treat.

"So let us give three hearty cheers
for little Orphan Ben, my dears."
They cheered, a most impressive noise
from one small girl and two small boys,
one belted knight, his lady too
and one fat gurgling child, "Goo goo!"

# VIII

## THE EPILOGUE

AND that's the end, except I'm sure
  you'd like to know a little more
  about the people who lived there
  at Number 14, Gloucester Square.
(The turkey, you'll be pleased to hear,
was found and roasted for New Year.)

Sir Hugh and Fanny Hertford Hare
  lived on in comfort in the Square,
  happy to give their grown up sons'
  and daughter's charming little-ones
  fantastic feasts at Christmastide;
  but in the end, alas!, they died.

Young Jack grew up and went to sea
and later, as a Captain, he
commanded ships and gave his best
in two world wars and on his chest
wore twenty medals, rather more
than any Hertford Hare before.

And Bert became an engineer
and did great things in Tanzania,
or Tanganyika as then was,
but often came back home because,
although he liked the place a lot,
he found the climate far too hot.

And what of little Annabel?
Ah yes!, of course, she married well.
Her husband's father was a peer.
She twice had twins within one year
and then she trained to be a vet
and was, what's more, a suffragette.

As for our hero, Orphan Ben,
he never had to sleep again
down in the coal-house with the cat,
he'd had more than his share of that.
Sir Hugh declared the boy no fool
and packed him off to boarding school.

And Ben enjoyed his education
which raised him miles above his station
so that in time he came to be
a Doctor of Philosophy
and in due course displayed such knowledge
they made him Master of his college.

And Marigold and Mrs Bold,
I can't be sure but I've been told,
went to the Isle of Wight near Cowes
and there they ran a boarding house
for many years through thick and thin
and never touched a drop of gin.

But now, about *that baby,* he,
you're right, it *was* a boy you see!,
was never told about the day
he landed on the roasting tray,
nor ever heard one single word
how he'd been taken for a bird.

His family thought, I'm sure with reason,
his little chums at school might seize on
this chance to call him silly names,
like *Flutterbum* or *Featherbrains*
which might have caused young Ned offence
and undermined his confidence.

So this *old* Ned knows not one thing,
his name's the same as that good king,
about the turkey and, what's more,
I know him well.  He lives next door,
still fit and frisky as I write,
at least he was last Friday night.

He was for years a city gent
and, for a while, in Parliament,
but now he's just an old, old man
I like to visit when I can,
and ev'ry single time I call
I'm shown a picture on his wall.

Says he, "This ancient photograph
is from *Strand Magazine*.  Don't laugh!,
for here is Arthur Balfour, see!,
and there's the king and, at his knee
are Jack and Bert and Annabel
and our dog Rover's there as well."

And then old Ned grows mighty proud
and speaks again but twice as loud,
"But that fat baby, do you see?
There in King Edward's arms, *that's me!*"
He jabs a finger near his ear
"Just think! My monarch kissed me here!"

"My king and emperor
kissed this
brow!"

But we know better,
don't we
now?

THE END